This book is dedicated to all the children I had the honor of teaching. I hope you learned life lessons from me, but more importantly, you felt cared about and loved. Being a teacher was one of my greatest joys! —TMT

To my loving family, thank you for always supporting my art, and to the little dreamers, may this book inspire you to reach for the stars and believe in your dreams. —JO

This edition first published in 2024
by Lawley Publishing,
a division of Lawley Enterprises LLC.

Text Copyright © 2024 by Terrilyn M. Trejo
Illustration Copyright © 2024 by Julia Olschanski
All Rights Reserved

Hardcover ISBN 978-1-960137-19-7
Paperback ISBN 978-1-960137-21-0
Library of Congress Control Number: 2023935684

Lawley Publishing
70 S. Val Vista Dr. #A3 #188
Gilbert, AZ 85296
LawleyPublishing.com

I LOVE America because . . .

Many extraordinary things have been invented here, like electricity, computers, the internet, and even video games. I'd love to be an inventor and design a flying car.

I LOVE America because . . .

You can meet many different types of people and learn from them. Yesterday, I met three new friends at the park. They taught me how to play the game Loteria. It's a bingo game from Mexico. Muchas gracias, amigos!

I LOVE
America because . . .

There are thousands of different books you can read! My most treasured book is Charlotte's Web. Charlotte, the spider, is such a good friend.

I LOVE America because . . .

You can explore many of our natural wonders, like the glaciers in Alaska, the California Redwoods, and even the Old Faithful geyser in Wyoming.

glaciers in Alaska

Grand Canyon

California Redwoods

Old Faithful Wyoming

Someday, I'd like to hike to the bottom of the Grand Canyon in Arizona.

I LOVE America because . . .

    I can go to school to learn how to write a paragraph, calculate fractions, and study the past in history class. But most of all, it's where I can be with all my friends. I have the most fantastic friends!

I LOVE America because . . .

PIZZA
Italy

CURRY
India

CROISSANT
France

TACO
Mexico

BURGER
USA

PRETZEL
Germany

There are so many different foods from many cultures around the world that I can try. I especially enjoy eating spicy Thai food.

THAI FOOD
Thailand

I can choose to celebrate lots of different holidays. My favorite holiday is the 4th of July. Watching fireworks in the night sky is always spectacular!

I LOVE America because . . .

I can travel to many exciting destinations. My favorite trip was visiting Yellowstone National Park and seeing the wild animals, especially the enormous Bison.

I LOVE
America because . . .

You can find so many fun things to keep yourself entertained, like seeing a movie, going to a concert, creating a beautiful piece of art, or just taking a hike in nature. My favorite form of entertainment is attending a school drama production. There are so many talented student actors!

I LOVE America because . . .

I can have a lemonade stand and make money to buy whatever I want. I'm saving my money to buy a shiny new bike.

I LOVE America because . . .

I am free to go to my church, or I can visit other places of worship. Recently, I was invited to a synagogue for a Bar Mitzvah. Mazel Tov!

I LOVE America because . . .

There are many people here to help me, protect me, and keep me safe. Today, a police officer talked to my class about "Stranger Danger," and the fire department helped create fire ecsape plans with us.

I LOVE America because . . .

When I am old enough, I can enlist in the military.
I think being a fighter pilot or becoming a Navy Seal
would be totally awesome!

I LOVE America because . . .

I can play any sport I desire if I practice and work really hard. I love playing soccer best of all!

I LOVE America because . . .

> I can grow up to have any career I can dream of, like being a chef, a video game designer, or a nurse. I sometimes dream of becoming the President of the United States of America. That would be a very important job.

. . . when I fall asleep at night, I know it's possible that many of my dreams can come true living here . . .

in America.

Printed in the USA
CPSIA information can be obtained
at www.ICGtesting.com
LVHW061916280224
772974LV00001B/1